TRICERATOPS

D0348287

TRICERATOPS FACT FILE

Triceratops was a type of dinosaur – part of a wider group called ceratopsians ('horn faces').

Length: **8–9m**

Height: **up to 3m**

Weight: **6–12 tonnes**

Top speed: **26km/h**

Number of teeth: **800**

Horn length: **up to 1m**

12368

Written by Susie Brooks

Illustrated by Jonathan Woodward

EGMONT
We bring stories to life

Book Band: White

First published in Great Britain 2016
by Egmont UK Limited
The Yellow Building, 1 Nicholas Road, London W11 4AN

www.egmont.co.uk

Text copyright © Egmont UK Limited 2016
Illustrations copyright © Jonathan Woodward 2016

Dinosaur consultancy by Professor Michael Benton

ISBN 978 1 4052 8042 6

A CIP catalogue record for this book is available from The British Library.

Printed in China
60657/1

Series ~~~~ **kki Gamble**

A DAY IN THE LIFE OF
TRICERATOPS

Reading Ladder

Contents

5 Introduction

6 Meet Triceratops

8 Triceratops teeth

10 Falling leaves

12 Toppling trees

14 Triceratops babies

16 Triceratops fight

18 Fancy frills

20 T. rex trouble

22 T. rex battle

24 The end of Triceratops

26 Dinosaur facts

28 Age of the dinosaurs

29 Why did the dinosaurs die out?

30 Pronunciation guide

31 Glossary

32 Index

Introduction

Many millions of years ago, the Earth was ruled by a rabble of roaring **reptiles** called dinosaurs.

Let's travel back in time to discover more about one of the most terrifying looking dinosaurs that ever lived.

Meet Triceratops

Triceratops had a huge head with three horns and a frightening frill around its neck.

Triceratops would have made a full-grown human look small.

Triceratops means
'three-horned face'.
You can see why!

Its beaky mouth worked
like scissors for snipping
off stems and leaves.

Triceratops teeth

Triceratops ate only plants. Luckily it was easy to find a tasty feast because trees, ferns and flowers were everywhere.

Triceratops had about 800 plant-grinding cheek teeth. They were arranged in rows and were replaced as they wore out.

◄ A Triceratops tooth had a flat edge.

◄ A T. rex tooth had a jagged edge, like a knife.

Falling leaves

Reaching the tall trees was tricky for Triceratops. It couldn't stretch up very far as it had stumpy legs and a heavy head.

Alamosaurus

Alamosaurus had better luck getting to the highest branches. Triceratops was ready to catch any leaves that dropped.

moth

beetle

ant

Beetles, moths, ants and other **insects**
lived alongside the dinosaurs.

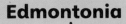

Edmontonia

Toppling trees

Down at ground level, there were plenty of plants to go around. Triceratops might have used its horns to topple taller plants, and Edmontonia was strong enough to barge trees over!

dragonfly

Triceratops babies

Like all dinosaurs, Triceratops hatched from an egg. Baby dinosaurs grew up fast, as long as a **carnivore** didn't munch them.

Bambiraptor

Triceratops laid its eggs in a nest and guarded them against thieving **raptors**, such as Bambiraptor.

Triceratops fight

Triceratops wasn't a carnivore, but it did know how to fight. The males probably locked horns with each other, to prove to the females who was the best!

Bone-headed Pachycephalosaurus
had a helmet-like skull, which it used
for either fighting or showing off.

Fancy frills

Another way to get the attention of the females was to put on a display. Triceratops probably flashed its fancy neck frill.

Its neck frill was as wide as a car!

The frill of a Triceratops
was a big fan-shaped bone,
covered in scaly skin.

frill

There are many things we think
Triceratops could have used its frill
for, such as:
- looking good
- looking terrifying
- protection in a fight
- keeping body temperature right

Tyrannosaurus rex was one of the deadliest carnivores ever to walk the Earth.

T. rex trouble

Some dinosaurs thundered around in a **herd** but Triceratops was often alone. This could mean trouble when danger crept up behind it, as Triceratops couldn't see over its own shoulder.

T. rex battle

When T. rex was hungry for a taste of Triceratops, there was nothing to do but fight. Who would win the battle? You decide!

Triceratops

Length: 8–9m
Weight: 6–12 tonnes
Top speed: 26km/h
Teeth: 800
Horns: 3

T. rex

Length: 12m

Weight: 6–7 tonnes

Top speed: 30km/h

Teeth: 60

Horns: 0

The end of Triceratops

About 66 million years ago the last of the dinosaurs died out. But we know they existed because dinosaur hunters have found lots of clues.

Fossil diggers have found many almost-complete **skeletons** of Triceratops.

The remains of dinosaurs are known as **fossils**. They include bones, teeth, skin, horns, eggs and even droppings!

In 2008, a Triceratops skeleton called
Cliff was sold to a dinosaur fan
for nearly one million US dollars!
The buyer donated it to the
Boston Museum of Science.

Stegosaurus

Triceratops didn't have a big
brain, but Stegosaurus had an even
smaller one. The brain of a Stegosaurus
was no bigger than a walnut.

**Quetzalcoatlus
(a pterosaur)**

While dinosaurs lived on land, giant reptiles called pterosaurs ruled the skies. Others, such as plesiosaurs, swam about in the oceans.

Kosmoceratops

Kosmoceratops had 15 full-size horns on its head.

Dinosaur facts

Age of the dinosaurs

The first dinosaurs appeared around 252 million years ago. Triceratops lived about 68–66 million years ago. This was during the Cretaceous Period.

Triassic Period
252–201 million years ago

Jurassic Period
201–145 million years ago

Cretaceous Period
145–66 million years ago

Why did the dinosaurs die out?

The dinosaurs died out after a massive space rock, or meteorite, crashed into Earth. It threw up dust clouds that blocked out the Sun, and the world became too cold for many living things to survive.

Pronunciation guide

Alamosaurus	AL-a-mo-SORE-us
Bambiraptor	BAM-bee-rap-tor
Edmontonia	ed-mon-TONE-ee-ah
Kosmoceratops	koz-mo-SERRA-tops
Pachycephalosaurus	pak-ee-SEF-uh-lo-SORE-us
Stegosaurus	STEG-oh-SORE-us
Triceratops	tri-SERRA-tops
Tyrannosaurus rex	tie-RAN-oh-SORE-us rex
Quetzalcoatlus	KWET-zal-koh-AT-lus

Glossary

carnivore   An animal that eats other animals.

fossils   Parts of an animal that have turned into rock.

herd   A large group of animals.

insects   Small creatures with six legs and a body formed of three parts, such as bees or ants.

raptors   Types of meat-eating dinosaurs that walked on two legs and had a large claw on each back foot.

reptiles   Cold-blooded animals that lay eggs and are covered in scales, such as lizards or dinosaurs.

skeleton   The framework of bones that supports the body of an animal or a human.

Index

Alamosaurus 11, 30

babies 15

Bambiraptor 15, 30

Edmontonia 13, 30

fighting 16–17, 22–23

fossils 24–25, 31

frills 6, 18–19

horns 6, 13, 16, 22, 25, 27

Kosmoceratops 27, 30

Pachycephalosaurus 17, 30

plesiosaurs 27

pterosaurs 27

Quetzalcoatlus 27, 30

skeletons 24, 26, 31

Stegosaurus 26, 30

teeth 9, 22, 23, 25

Tyrannosaurus rex 9, 20, 22–23, 30